Pinky Doodle Dance

Elizabeth Hamilton-Guarino and Kris Fuller

To Lev
Happy Birthday!

Published by Waldorf Publishing
2140 Hall Johnson Road
#102-345
Grapevine, Texas 76051
www.WaldorfPublishing.com

Pinky Doodle Dance

ISBN: 978-1-68524-647-1

Library of Congress Control Number: 2020948870

Copyright © 2021

Illustrations by Vova Kirichenko
Design by Baris Celik

For Peter, Connor, Quinn, Cam, Quaid, Ben, and Mia.

The forest is buzzing with all sorts of cheer.
The Pinky Doodle Dance will soon be here!

Pinky can't wait for all of the fun-
Costumes, sparkles, and dancing a ton.

FOREST
DANCE
PARTY

Decorations, invites, and music will play—
streamers and beautiful lights on display.

The forest will twinkle like stars in the sky.
"There's so much to do!" Pinky says. "Oh my!"

"I'm here to help," chimes Fred the Fox.
"Hooray!" cheers Pinky. "Unpack this box!"

"It's beautiful lights and strings that all glow,
but how they got tangled, I'll never know."

Murphy the Moose hears Pinky's cry.
He gallops over, "I'm here! I'm your guy!"

"That's great," smiles Pinky. "You came in a flash."
In the next moment they hear a huge crash!

KA
BOOM!

Poor Fred is tangled. He's wrapped up in lights.
He could sure use a hand (or an antler) all right.

Murphy leans down and scoops up some cable,
"Step left. No, go right. Duck! If you're able."

Fred smiles at Pinky, "Please don't worry.
We'll have this untangled and up in a hurry."

"That's right," chuckles Murphy as he looks at the sight.
"Baxter will make sure everything's right."

Sally the Spider swings in on her threads.
She's high in the branches above all their heads.

"Please hang the streamers way up in the trees."
"You've got it, Pinky. That is a breeze!"

The birds arrive chirping, "Here we are!
We'll fly through the forest, near and far."
"That's great," smiles Pinky. "The dance is tonight.
Invite the whole forest. It will be a delight."

The birds fly away with their fluttering song:
"The dance is tonight! Everyone, come along!"

With the help of her friends, preparations are done.

It's time to get ready. It's time for some fun!

Porcupine Pete is a sharply dressed critter.
"I love shiny shoes and suspenders with glitter!"

Baxter the Bee does ballet, jazz, and tap.
He buzzes around in a shiny, pink cap.

Pinky's dress sparkles so much that it glows.
It's covered in sequins, pink ribbons, and bows!

The music begins with a fast and fun beat.
The stick bugs play drums and stomp their stick feet.

Pinky's excited because now is her chance—
to jump and doodle and shine at the dance.

Olive and Oscar are next to arrive.
These owls dressed up and they know how to jive!

They wear fancy outfits – bright purple and blue.
Their shoes are sparkly and they sing "Hoo-Hoo!"

Pete the Porcupine taps to and fro.
Fred the Fox is ready to go!

Clara the Caterpillar just can't stop.
Benji and Betty do their best bunny hop.

Sally the Spider's eight legs keep the beat.
It's amazing to watch her fast moving feet.

Murphy the Moose gets his time to shine.
His breakdancing moves are incredibly fine!

The Doodle Dance goes late into the night.

The creatures all groove in the golden moonlight.

They disco, they limbo, they tip, and they tap.
While lightning bugs shimmer above – Zip, Zip, Zap!

They dip, dive and tango for one final chance.
It's almost the end of their fabulous dance.

At midnight it's over. The dance party ends.
It's late now for Pinky and all of her friends.

They clean up together. They turn down the light.

Let Your Dreams Fly!

It's time to dream now. Go to bed and sleep tight.

The End.
But not the end of
Pinky's Adventures...

Doodle Pages

Doodle Pages

Doodle Pages

CPSIA information can be obtained
at www.ICGtesting.com
Printed in the USA
LVHW070034030122
707686LV00002B/3